Adapted by David Lewman
Illustrated by Craig Kellman

SECRET LIFE OF PETS: DELUXE STORYBOOK
A CENTUM BOOK 9781910916544
Published in Great Britain by Centum Books Ltd
This edition published 2016
© 2016 Universal Studios Licensing LLC.
1 3 5 7 9 10 8 6 4 2
The Secret Life of Pets is a trademark and copyright of Universal Studios. Licensed by Universal Studios Licensing LLC. All rights reserved.

Centum Books Ltd, 20 Devon Square, Newton Abbot, Devon TQ12 2HR, UK
books@centumbooksltd.co.uk
CENTUM BOOKS Limited Reg. No. 07641486
A CIP catalogue record for this book is available from the British Library
Printed in China.

Hi! My name is Max. I'm the luckiest dog in the whole world. I live in New York City with my owner, Katie. She's the greatest! We have the perfect relationship. She'd do anything for me. And I'm her loyal protector.

Even when I make little mistakes, Katie understands that I'm not perfect, so she always forgives me. Our love is stronger than words . . . **or shoes**.

By the way, Katie has great taste in shoes. And her shoes taste great!

It's me and Katie. Katie and me. Us against the world.
No matter what comes our way. Together we can handle
whatever life throws at us. That's how it is, and that's
how we like it!

There's just one little problem with our relationship.
Pretty much every day, Katie leaves. Sometimes I try stuff
to get her to stay. I do all my best tricks.

I miss her so much while she's gone. All day, I sit by the
front door of our apartment, waiting for her to come back.

Well, actually, I don't sit by the front door *all* day. Luckily, I have other friends who live in our apartment building and the building next door. They're pets like me. Most days they come to visit. We all miss our owners during the day, but at least we can keep each other company.

GIDGET is a Pomeranian. She lives in the building across the way. A Pomeranian looks like someone made a little dog out of cotton wool. Every morning, Gidget jumps up onto a pillow by her window and calls across to me.

Gidget always asks me what my plans for the day are. She thinks my life is very exciting. She must, because she spends her whole day staring at me.

CHLOE the cat is always there for me when I need some good advice. She's really smart. All I have to do to visit her is go out of our window and climb up the fire escape to the apartment Chloe lives in. Sometimes she comes down to my place.

But lately she's been having a little trouble squeezing through the window. You see, Chloe likes human food.

LOTS of human food. I think it must be a cat thing. As a dog, I stay focused on Katie coming home – but cats . . . cats do what cats do, I guess.

SWEETPEA is a little bird called a budgie. But don't let his size fool you. His body may be small, but his imagination is big!

OFF
FAN ON

As soon as his owner leaves in the morning, Sweetpea likes to turn on a fan and a video of fighter jets zooming through a canyon . . .

CLICK!

. . . and then he flies right in front of the TV screen,
pretending he's a fighter jet, too!

VROOOOM!

MEL is a pug. He's a big fan of pillows (for chewing), balls (for chasing) and delicious peanut butter (for eating). But there's one thing he definitely does not like at all – squirrels!

He thinks that squirrels are going to try to take over the world.
I think he's wrong about that. But he is right about peanut butter.

LEONARD is a poodle. He lives in a fancy apartment. Looking at him, you might think he's kind of snobby, like his owner. But after his owner leaves for the day, telling him to be a good boy . . .

. . . Leonard pushes a button on the stereo with his nose to play loud, thumping, hard-rocking music! He and his friends shake their heads and shout along with the songs! Leonard definitely knows how to cut loose and **ROCK!**

BUDDY is a dachshund. He loves having his long body massaged. As soon as his owner heads out for the day, Buddy hurries into the kitchen. He jumps up on the counter, knocks the bowl off the mixer, and flips the switch.

WHIRRR!

PARIS

When I look up, I often see **NORMAN** the guinea pig peeking through the vents in our apartment. He got lost in the heating ducts and hasn't been able to find his way home yet, but he never gives up. Good luck, Norman.

And then there's **POPS**. Since his owner is never at home, everyone likes to hang out at his place. It's a real pet hot spot.

Don't worry about Pops's wheels – this old basset hound gets around fine. In fact, he's been around so long, he knows everyone in New York.

As you can see, my life is pretty sweet. I get to spend the day with my friends, and then comes my very favourite moment – when Katie returns home and it's just the two of us again. We are a perfect team, with exactly two members, taking on the world together.

Hey, here's Katie now! And she's brought me a surprise! That is just like her! She's so great!

It's a ...

It's a ...

Let's learn MORE about Max and his friends!

MAX

Hi! My name is Max. I love my owner, Katie. I can't wait for her to come home to play. When she's not home, I hang out with my pet friends in an apartment building in New York City.

DUKE

My name is Duke. Katie adopted me. Now I'm Max's new brother. I don't think Max liked me at first. I don't know why.

SECRET THOUGHT:

I like sharing – especially with Max.

GIDGET

I'm Max's next-door neighbour, Gidget. Max doesn't know this, but I have a huge crush on him. I'd do anything for Max.

SECRET THOUGHT:
I
LOVE
MAX

CHLOE

I'm Chloe. I love food. When I'm not eating, I am giving priceless advice to Max and the other pets in the building. Not that they listen and not that I care.

Chloe

My pet pals aren't so bad, but I would never admit it.

MEL

I'm Mel. I love to run around and chase things – especially squirrels. I must keep my owner safe from them.

SECRET THOUGHT:

Squirrels –they're going to take over the world!

BUDDY

Hi! My name is Buddy.
I'm a Dachshund, and
when I'm not hanging out
with my best friend, Mel,
I love a good belly rub.

SECRET THOUGHT:

I'm the coolest dog on
the entire block.

We LOVE our owners and they love us!